WHY I DEFEND APOSTLE PAUL

Rightly Dividing Scripture and the Gospel of Grace

William A. Orr Jr

Page Intentionally Left Blank.

Dedication

This book is lovingly dedicated to my wife, **Laura**, and to my three beautiful children with her **Barrett, Gianna, and Petra.**

To my second wife, **Loni,** who is now in Heaven, and to my first wife, **Linda**, and her husband **Boyd.**

To my oldest daughter **Rebecca** and her mother **Colleen,** and to Rebecca's sons **Patrick** and **Dylan.**

To my daughter **Kelly** and her husband **Gary**, and their two children, **Ashlyn** and **Austin.**

To my son **Billy** and his wife **Tara**, and their two children, **Kaitlyn** and **Billy.**

To my daughter **Brittney** and her partner **Devin**, and her son **Sawyer.**

To my daughter **Kristen** and her fiancé **Ralph**, and their daughter **Sailor Grey.**

To my daughter **Kaycee** and her partner **Anthony,** and their daughters **Cruize, Tatum** and their soon-to-be little blessing, **Lonnie Jane.**

To my sister **Carla** and her husband **Mike,** and their children **Adrienne** (and her husband **Kyle,** and their daughters **Quinn** and **Marlee**) and **Jason** (and his wife **Kara Sue** and their daughter **Bella**).

To my sisters-in-law **Julie** and **Linell,** and to my niece **Cassie.**

To all my **Bible Study friends in Plattsburgh, New York, and Lakewood Ranch, Florida,** who continue to help me grow in God's Word and truth.

Finally, **to Les Feldick,** my teacher in scripture for the last fourteen years.

This book is a testimony to God's grace and to the power of His Word rightly divided.

Table of Contents

Preface

My journey has been far from perfect, but through it all, the hand of God has guided me even when I didn't realize it.

I grew up in Witherbee, New York, in a small town where, in my eyes, I was at the center of everything, running bars, drinking, doing drugs, gambling, and living a sinner's life. I went back and forth in my faith for years. I believed in Christ but didn't understand what it meant to truly live for Him.

In my twenties, a close friend told me about being "born again." I believed in Jesus, but thought I already had it all figured out. I even tried to prove my friend wrong. I was blind, thinking I knew the truth when I really didn't.

Through sin, selfishness, and worldly living, I had no idea how deeply I would one day depend on the grace of God. My second wife, Loni, passed away at age 34, leaving me with three daughters, just days before 9/11. My first day back at work after burying her was the morning of that terrible day.

Years later, in 2017, I faced my greatest trial yet: stage four kidney cancer. The cancer had spread into my vena cava, just a half inch from my heart. The operation lasted about eight hours. My body was cooled down to 68°, and I was clinically dead for 45 minutes while a heart surgeon and a kidney surgeon worked side by side to save me. They had only a 45-minute window to remove the cancer before warming my body back up. But by God's grace, I lived.

Three years later, I was diagnosed again with stage four metastatic renal cell carcinoma and developed a large tumor in my pelvis. I underwent 15 radiation treatments. Though I felt no pain, the effects of the medication later caused ONJ (osteonecrosis of the jaw), killing part of my jawbone. Yet even through that, I still felt God's presence with me.

I live with diabetes today, but I feel good because my faith gives me strength. I believe that through every trial, God was shaping me to help others, to share my testimony, and to spread the truth of His Word, especially through the ministry of the Apostle Paul.

This book is written from the conviction that God revealed through Paul a message for our time, the dispensation of grace, and that we must not mix the Gospel of the Kingdom given to Israel with the Gospel of Grace given to the Body of Christ.

It is my prayer that through these words, someone will come to see the truth that changed my life, that Jesus Christ died for our sins, was buried, and rose again, and that faith alone in that finished work brings salvation.

Opening Scriptures

Before beginning, a few verses frame the truth of this book:

Deuteronomy 29:29 (KJV)

"The secret things belong unto the LORD our God: but those things which are revealed belong unto us and to our children for ever, that we may do all the words of this law."

Luke 18:31, 32, 33, 34 (KJV)

*"31 Then he took the 12 aside and said to them. "Behold, we are going up to Jerusalem, and all things which are written through the prophets about the Son of Man will be accomplished. 32 For he will be handed over to the Gentiles, and will be mocked and mistreated and spat upon. 33 and after they have scourged Him, they will kill him, and the third day He will rise again." 34 **And they understood none of these things: and this saying was hid from them, neither knew they the things which were spoken.**"*

These verses remind us that God reveals truth in His time and that even the apostles didn't fully understand Christ's purpose until after His resurrection. In this same way, the full mystery of the Body of Christ was later revealed through Paul.

2 Timothy 2:15; 3:16 (KJV)

"Study to shew thyself approved unto God, a workman that needeth not to be ashamed, rightly dividing the word of truth. All scripture is given by inspiration of God, and is profitable for doctrine, for reproof, for correction, for instruction in righteousness."

CHAPTER 1

The Call of Paul

Few figures in Scripture have caused as much misunderstanding - or carry as much importance for today's believers - as the Apostle Paul. He was chosen by Christ Himself, after the resurrection, to bring forth a new revelation: the Gospel of Grace to the Gentiles and the Body of Christ.

Before his conversion, Paul (then called Saul) was a fierce persecutor of the Christians - zealous for the law and convinced he was defending God's truth. Yet, it was this man, the least likely candidate, that God would use to deliver the most important message of all: that salvation is now by grace through faith alone, not of works or law.

Scripture: Acts 9:1-6 (KJV)

> *"And Saul, yet breathing out threatenings and slaughter against the disciples of the Lord this, went unto the high priest,*

And desired of him letters to Damascus to the synagogues, that if he found any of this way, whether they were men or women, he might bring them bound unto Jerusalem.

And as he journeyed, he came near Damascus: and suddenly there shone round about him a light from heaven: And he fell to the earth, and heard a voice saying unto him, Saul, Saul, why persecutest thou me?

And he said, Who art thou, Lord? And the Lord said, I am Jesus whom thou persecutest: it is hard for thee to kick against these pricks.

And he, trembling and astonished, said, Lord, what wilt thou have me to do?"

Explanation:

In that moment, the risen Christ appeared not in weakness, as He had before the cross, but in glory. Paul's conversion marked the beginning of a new dispensation - not under law, but under grace.

The Lord did not send Paul to continue the ministry of Peter and the Twelve to Israel; He sent him with an entirely new message - to reveal the mystery hidden since the world began.

This was not just a change of mission - it was a change in the way God would deal with mankind.

Scripture: Acts 9:15 (KJV)

> "But the Lord said unto him, Go thy way: for he is a **chosen vessel** unto me, to bear my name before the Gentiles, and kings and the children of Israel."

Explanation:

Here, Jesus Himself declares Paul's divine purpose - to bear His name before the Gentiles.

This is not something said of Peter of the Twelve. Their mission was to Israel - to offer the Kingdom promised to Abraham, Isaac, and Jacob.

Paul's mission was heavenly - to form a spiritual body, the Church, composed of Jew and Gentile alike, saved by grace through faith alone.

Scripture: Galatians 1:11-12 (KJV)

> "But I certify you, brethren, that the gospel which was preached of me is not after man.
>
> For I neither received it of man, neither was I taught it, but by the revelation of Jesus Christ."

Explanation:

Paul emphasizes that the message he preached - salvation by grace through faith - came directly from the risen Lord, not from any man, not even the Twelve Apostles.

This gospel, distinct from the Gospel of the Kingdom, was a revelation of the risen Christ to Paul alone.

That's why Paul often refers to it as "my gospel" (Romans 2:16; 16:25; 2 Timothy 2:8) - not out of pride but to mark it as a new revelation given specifically to him for this age of grace.

Scripture: 1 Timothy 1:12-16 (KJV)

> *"And I thank Christ Jesus our Lord, who hath enabled me, for that he counted me faithful, putting me into the ministry;*
>
> *Who was before a blasphemer, and a persecutor, and injurious: but I obtained mercy, because I did it ignorantly in unbelief.*
>
> *And the grace of our Lord was exceeding abundant with faith and love which is in Christ Jesus.*
>
> *This is a faithful saying, and worthy of all acceptation, that Christ Jesus came into the world to save sinners; of whom I am chief.*
>
> *Howbeit for this cause I obtained mercy, that in me first Jesus Christ might shew forth all longsuffering, for a pattern to them which should hereafter believe on him to life everlasting."*

Explanation:

Paul describes himself as the chief of sinners, yet chosen by Christ as a pattern for all who would believe afterward.

The word first here ("**in me first**") marks Paul as the first member of the Body of Christ - the prototype of God's grace extended to all sinners.

Paul's conversion on the road to Damascus was therefore not the beginning of the Church of Pentecost, but the beginning of something entirely new - the Body of Christ.

Scripture: 1 Corinthians 3:10 (KJV)

> *"According to the grace of God which is given unto me, as a wise masterbuilder, I have laid the foundation, and another buildeth thereon, but let every man take heed how he buildeth thereupon."*

Explanation:

Here, Paul calls himself a masterbuilder - the one who laid the foundation for the Church.

That foundation is not Peter or any man, but Christ revealed through Paul's Gospel.

This is why the modern Church must return to Paul's teachings - because they are the marching orders for believers today in this dispensation of grace.

Paul's writings (Romans through Philemon) form the blueprint for how we live, walk, and serve under grace - not under law.

Reflection:

When we see Paul's calling for what it is - a personal commission from the risen Christ to reveal a new gospel of grace - everything in Scripture starts to make sense.

The law was holy, but it condemned us. Grace saves us.

Israel was promised an earthly kingdom.

The Body of Christ is promised a heavenly inheritance.

Peter and the Twelve looked for Christ's return to earth; Paul looked for our gathering in heaven.

Scripture: Romans 16:25 (KJV)

> *"Now to him that is of power to establish you according to my gospel, and the preaching of Jesus Christ, according to the revelation of the mystery, which was kept secret since the world began."*

Explanation:

Notice, Paul calls it my gospel.

This isn't pride, it's distinction.

He was entrusted with a unique revelation that had been kept secret until the proper time.

And this mystery is what "establishes" the believer, gives us strength, peace, and assurance in Christ.

That's why understanding Paul's message isn't optional; it's essential to walking in the grace God intended for His Church.

Reflection:

The mystery revealed through Paul is the greatest truth of the Church Age.

It's the key that unlocks the rest of Scripture.

It shows us that we're not Israel, we're a heavenly people with a heavenly destiny.

Our hope isn't an earthly kingdom, but to be caught up to meet the Lord in the air and be with Him forever.

This revelation was not an afterthought; it was God's plan all along, hidden until the time was right.

And when it was revealed to Paul, it became the cornerstone of the Gospel of Grace, the good news that salvation is complete, finished, and freely given to all who believe.

CHAPTER 2

𝓣𝓱𝓮 𝓣𝔀𝓸 𝓖𝓸𝓼𝓹𝓮𝓵𝓼 𝓛𝓪𝔀 &

𝓖𝓻𝓪𝓬𝓮

From the very beginning, God's plan for humanity has always been one of redemption. But the way He revealed that plan changed as history moved forward.

In the Old Testament and through the earthly ministry of Jesus, God dealt primarily with Israel under the Law.

But through the Apostle Paul, He revealed something brand new, the Gospel of Grace, for all nations, apart from the Law.

Scripture: John 1:17 (KJV)

"For the law was given by Moses, but grace and truth came by Jesus Christ."

Explanation:

This verse lays the foundation. The Law, given through Moses, demanded perfect obedience. It showed mankind's sinfulness and need for a Savior, but it could never give life.

Grace, however, came by Jesus Christ. Grace does what the Law never could; it saves sinners freely by faith.

But here's the key:

Jesus did not reveal the full message of grace during His earthly ministry.

He came to fulfill the Law and offer the Kingdom to Israel first.

Scripture: Matthew 15:24 (KJV)

> *"But he answered and said, I am not sent but unto the lost sheep of the house of Israel."*

Explanation:

Jesus' ministry in the four Gospels was directed to Israel. He healed their sick, preached repentance, and proclaimed that the Kingdom of Heaven was at hand.

This was the message of the Gospel of the Kingdom, the good news that the long-promised Messiah had come to establish His rule on earth through Israel.

When Israel rejected that message and crucified their King, God temporarily set aside His program with Israel and began something new, a mystery hidden since the foundation of the world.

That's when Christ revealed Himself to Paul, ushering in the Gospel of Grace.

Scripture: Galatians 2:7 (KJV)

> *"But contrariwise, when they saw that the gospel of the uncircumcision was committed unto me, as the gospel of the circumcision was unto Peter;"*

Explanation:

This verse makes it clear: there were two distinct gospels operating for a time.

- Peter preached the Gospel of the Circumcision, the message of repentance, and the coming earthly Kingdom to Israel.
- Paul preached the Gospel of the Uncircumcision, the message of salvation by grace through faith, to all nations.

Both were true for their time, but only Paul's gospel applies to the Church today.

When Israel rejected Christ again after His resurrection (Acts 7, the stoning of Stephen), God turned to the Gentiles through Paul.

Scripture: Ephesians 2:8–9 (KJV)

> *"For by grace are ye saved through faith; and that not of yourselves: it is the gift of God, Not of works, lest any man should boast."*

Explanation:

This is the heart of the Gospel of Grace: salvation is a gift, completely apart from works, law, or rituals.

Under the Law, blessings came through obedience; under Grace, blessings come through belief.

Paul's message wasn't about reforming human behavior; it was about transforming the heart through faith in Christ's finished work on the cross.

Scripture: Romans 6:14 (KJV)

> *"For sin shall not have dominion over you: for ye are not under the law, but under grace."*

Explanation:

Under the Law, sin ruled because the Law constantly exposed our failures.

Under Grace, sin's power is broken because Christ's righteousness is credited to us.

We don't earn God's favor; we live in it because we're in Christ.

This is the key truth most churches overlook today.

Too often, they mix Law and Grace, teaching believers to strive, perform, and fear losing salvation, instead of resting in what Christ has already done.

Paul's Distinct Message:

Paul's revelation completes the Word of God for this dispensation.

He was given mysteries that had been hidden truths not known by Moses, David, or even the Twelve apostles during Christ's earthly ministry.

"Even the mystery which hath been hid from ages and from generations, but now is made manifest to his saints" Colossians 1:26 (KJV)

This "mystery" was that Jew and Gentile would be made one body in Christ, seated in heavenly places, not an earthly kingdom, but a heavenly calling.

Reflection:

When you rightly divide the Word (2 Timothy 2:15), everything begins to fit:

- The Gospel of the Kingdom (through Peter and the Twelve) looked forward to Christ ruling on earth.
- The Gospel of Grace (through Paul) looks upward to our heavenly position in Christ.

One gospel required repentance, baptism, and enduring to the end.

The other offers immediate salvation by faith alone in Christ alone.

That's why Paul could boldly say:

"Be ye followers of me, even as I also am of Christ." 1 Corinthians 11:1 (KJV)

Because Paul followed the risen, glorified Christ the same One who now sits at the right hand of God.

CHAPTER 3

The Mystery Revealed

When God revealed His plan of salvation to Paul, He unveiled something that had been hidden from the foundation of the world.

It was a divine secret, a "mystery" not made known to any of the prophets or apostles before him.

This mystery changed everything about how God deals with mankind.

It revealed a brand-new relationship between heaven and earth, one not built on Israel's covenants or the Law, but on grace alone.

Scripture: Ephesians 3:2–6 (KJV)

> *"If ye have heard of the dispensation of the grace of God which is given me to you-ward:*

How that by revelation he made known unto me the mystery; (as I wrote afore in few words, Whereby, when ye read, ye may understand my knowledge in the mystery of Christ)

Which in other ages was not made known unto the sons of men, as it is now revealed unto his holy apostles and prophets by the Spirit;

That the Gentiles should be fellowheirs, and of the same body, and partakers of his promise in Christ by the gospel."

Explanation:

Paul says plainly that this "dispensation of grace" was given to him for us.

That means the gospel we live under today, salvation by grace through faith, was not revealed before Paul's ministry.

This mystery was that Jew and Gentile would now be one body in Christ, seated in heavenly places, not an earthly kingdom, but a spiritual one.

Under the old program, Israel was God's chosen nation.

Under grace, there is no difference between Jew and Gentile.

Scripture: Galatians 3:28 (KJV)

"There is neither Jew nor Greek, there is neither bond nor free, there is neither male nor female for ye are all one in Christ Jesus."

Explanation:

In God's new creation, earthly distinctions disappear.

Every believer, regardless of background, race, or status, becomes part of the same Body of Christ.

This truth was never prophesied in the Old Testament.

The prophets saw a Messiah reigning from Jerusalem, restoring Israel, and ruling over all nations, but they did not see a heavenly body of believers united in grace.

Paul's Revelation Was Unique

Paul's gospel did not come from men, nor did he learn it from the Twelve apostles.

It came directly from the risen, glorified Christ.

Scripture: Galatians 1:11–12 (KJV)

> *"But I certify you, brethren, that the gospel which was preached of me is not after man, For I neither received it of man, neither was I taught it, but by the revelation of Jesus Christ."*

Explanation:

When Paul met Christ on the road to Damascus (Acts 9), he wasn't just converted; he was commissioned.

The Lord revealed to him a new truth, a message never before preached:

That Christ's death and resurrection were not just for Israel, but for the whole world, and that faith alone was now the key to salvation.

This was the "mystery of Christ," the secret of how God would save sinners apart from works, rituals, or the Law, uniting them into one spiritual body destined for heaven.

Scripture: Colossians 1:25–27 (KJV)

"Whereof I am made a minister, according to the dispensation of God which is given to me for you, to fulfil the word of God; Even the mystery which hath been hid from ages and from generations, but now is made manifest to his saints: To whom God would make known what is the riches of the glory of this mystery among the Gentiles; which is Christ in you, the hope of glory."

Explanation:

This passage is one of the most beautiful summaries of Paul's message.

He says this mystery "fulfills" the Word of God, meaning it completes the divine revelation.

What had been hidden through all generations is now revealed: Christ in you, not just among you, the indwelling presence of the risen Savior in every believer.

This truth transforms our relationship with God.

We are not waiting for His Spirit to come upon us, as in the Old Testament, He already lives within us.

That's the hope and glory of the Christian life.

The Mystery vs. Prophecy:

To understand your Bible clearly, you must separate what was prophesied from what was revealed.

CHAPTER 4

Paul's Conversion And Commission

The story of the Apostle Paul is one of the most powerful testimonies in all of Scripture.

It's a story of mercy, transformation, and purpose. A man once devoted to destroying the name of Jesus became the very one chosen to spread His gospel of grace.

Paul's conversion marks the beginning of a brand-new dispensation, the start of God's direct outreach to the Gentiles.

This is where the "Body of Christ" begins.

Scripture: Acts 9:1–6 (KJV)

"And Saul, yet breathing out threatenings and slaughter against the disciples of the Lord, went unto the high priest, And desired of him letters to Damascus to the synagogues, that if he found any of this way, whether they were men or women, he might bring them bound unto Jerusalem.

And as he journeyed, he came near Damascus: and suddenly there shone round about him a light from heaven, and he fell to the earth, and heard a voice saying unto him, Saul, Saul, why persecutest thou me?

And he said, Who art thou, Lord? And the Lord said, I am Jesus whom thou persecutest: it is hard for thee to kick against the pricks.

And he, trembling and astonished, said, Lord, what wilt thou have me to do? And the Lord said unto him, Arise, and go into the city, and it shall be told thee what thou must do."

Explanation:

Before his conversion, Saul of Tarsus was a devout Pharisee zealous for the Law, but blind to the truth.

He sincerely believed he was serving God by persecuting those who followed Jesus.

But on that road to Damascus, everything changed.

The risen, glorified Christ personally appeared to him not from earth, but from heaven.

This was the first time in Scripture that Christ spoke from His heavenly position to a human being.

It was not the Jesus of Nazareth walking the dusty roads of Galilee, but the ascended Lord, now seated at the right hand of God.

And from that moment, Paul's entire life and human history took a turn.

The Turning Point in God's Program

At that point, God temporarily set Israel aside in unbelief (Romans 11:25).

The prophetic program paused, and a new one began, the mystery program through Paul.

The kingdom promised to Israel was postponed.

Instead, God opened the door to the Gentiles through grace, not by works, covenants, or law, but through faith alone in the finished work of the cross.

Paul became the "pattern" for all who would believe after him.

Scripture: 1 Timothy 1:15 16 (KJV)

> *"This is a faithful saying, and worthy of all acceptation, that Christ Jesus came into the world to save sinners; of whom I am chief. Howbeit for this cause I obtained mercy, that in me first Jesus Christ might shew forth all longsuffering, for a*

pattern to them which should hereafter believe on him to life everlasting."

Explanation

Paul didn't just receive mercy; he became an example of it.

In him, God displayed His perfect patience toward sinners.

If He could save Saul, the persecutor, He can save anyone.

Paul says, "in me first," showing he was the first person saved under this new dispensation, the Gospel of Grace.

From that point on, salvation would come not by joining Israel or keeping the Law, but by believing in Christ's death, burial, and resurrection (1 Corinthians 15:1–4).

Christ's Direct Calling

Later, when Paul recounted his testimony before King Agrippa, he explained what Jesus told him that day:

Scripture: Acts 26:16 18 (KJV)

"But rise, and stand upon thy feet: for I have appeared unto thee for this purpose, to make thee a minister and a witness both of these things which thou hast seen,

and of those things in which I will appear unto thee;

Delivering thee from the people, and from the Gentiles, unto whom now I send thee,

To open their eyes, and to turn them from darkness to light, and from the power of Satan unto God, that they may receive forgiveness of sins, and inheritance among them which are sanctified by faith that is in me."

Explanation:

Here, Jesus commissions Paul as His chosen messenger to the Gentiles.

He tells him plainly, "unto whom now I send thee."

This is the first time God formally sends someone directly to the Gentiles with a message of salvation by faith alone.

Paul would later confirm this again in Galatians 2:7-9, where Peter, James, and John agreed that he would go to the uncircumcision (Gentiles) while they continued ministering to the circumcision (Jews).

Paul: The Master Builder

Paul often described his ministry in terms of building a foundation that no one else had laid before.

Scripture: 1 Corinthians 3:10–11 (KJV)

"According to the grace of God which is given unto me, as a wise masterbuilder, I have laid the foundation, and another buildeth thereon. But let every man take heed how he buildeth thereupon. For other foundation can no man lay than that which is laid, which is Jesus Christ."

Explanation:

Paul was the "master builder" of the Church, not its founder (Christ is that), but the one through whom the Lord revealed its blueprint.

His writings show us how the Body of Christ should function, grow, and live by grace.

We are all builders on that foundation Christ Himself, but we must build carefully, with truth and faithfulness, not tradition or human wisdom.

Reflection:

Paul's conversion shows the boundless mercy of God and the complete change in His dealings with mankind.

Through Paul, the Lord revealed a new relationship not based on Israel's promises, but on personal faith in Christ's finished work.

Every believer today owes their salvation to the message God gave Paul, the Gospel of Grace.

That's why understanding his calling is so vital: without Paul, we would still be lost in religious confusion, trying to earn what can only be freely given.

CHAPTER 5

The Order of Events
From Cross to Rapture

Understanding the order of events after Christ's death and resurrection is one of the most important keys to rightly dividing the Word of Truth.

It helps us see where we fit in God's plan, how His dealings with humanity have changed, and what awaits us in the future.

This chapter follows the sequence from the Cross, to the resurrection, to the call of Paul, to the rapture of the Church, and shows how God revealed His plan step by step.

The Crucifixion and Resurrection of Christ

The foundation of everything begins at the Cross.

When Jesus died, He paid the full penalty for sin once and for all.

Then, through His resurrection, He conquered death itself.

Scripture: 1 Corinthians 15:3–4 (KJV)

> *"For I delivered unto you first of all that which I also received, how that Christ died for our sins according to the scriptures; And that he was buried, and that he rose again the third day according to the scriptures."*

Explanation:

Paul summarizes the entire gospel in two verses.

The death, burial, and resurrection of Christ is not just history; it is the power of God unto salvation for everyone who believes (Romans 1:16).

The Cross marked the end of the old covenant and the beginning of the new era of grace.

No longer would forgiveness come through animal sacrifices or temple rituals but through the finished work of the Lamb of God.

The Coming of the Holy Spirit at Pentecost

After Jesus ascended, the Holy Spirit came upon the apostles in Jerusalem.

This was the birth of the believing Jewish assembly, empowered to proclaim Jesus as the risen Messiah to the nation of Israel.

Scripture: Acts 2:36 38 (KJV)

"Therefore, let all the house of Israel know assuredly, that God hath made that same Jesus, whom ye have crucified, both Lord and Christ.

Now when they heard this, they were pricked in their heart, and said unto Peter and to the rest of the apostles, Men and brethren, what shall we do?

Then Peter said unto them, Repent, and be baptized every one of you in the name of Jesus Christ for the remission of sins, and ye shall receive the gift of the Holy Ghost."

Explanation:

Peter's message was still directed to Israel.

He preached repentance and baptism as part of Israel's national call to accept their Messiah.

At this point, the "Body of Christ" was not yet revealed.

God was still offering the kingdom to Israel just as Jesus had promised the twelve apostles (Matthew 19:28).

But the nation as a whole rejected that offer.

Israel's Continued Rejection

Even after the miracles and the Spirit's outpouring, Israel's leaders refused to believe.

Stephen's speech in Acts 7 was the final national rejection.

Scripture: Acts 7:51–52 (KJV)

"Ye stiffnecked and uncircumcised in heart and ears, ye do always resist the Holy Ghost: as your fathers did, so do ye. Which of the prophets have not your fathers persecuted? And they have slain them which shewed before of the coming of the Just One; of whom ye have been now the betrayers and murderers."

Explanation:

When Stephen was stoned, Israel effectively said "no" to the Holy Spirit's witness.

At that moment, God began to turn away from His prophetic program with Israel and began preparing a new revelation.

The next chapter, Acts 9, introduces Saul of Tarsus, the man who would become the Apostle Paul.

The Conversion of Paul: The New Dispensation Begins

God chose Paul to introduce something never before known or revealed:

The Gospel of Grace and the formation of the Body of Christ.

Scripture: Ephesians 3:2–5, 9 (KJV)

> *"If ye have heard of the dispensation of the grace of God which is given me to you-ward: How that by revelation he made known unto me the mystery;*
>
> *(as I wrote afore in a few words, whereby, when ye read, ye may understand my knowledge in the mystery of Christ)*
>
> *Which in other ages was not made known unto the sons of men... And to make all men see what is the fellowship of the mystery, which from the beginning of the world hath been hid in God."*

Explanation:

Through Paul, God revealed His secret plan hidden from all previous generations that Jew and Gentile would now be united in one body, not by law, but by grace through faith.

This is the present "church age," often called "the dispensation of grace."

We are saved not by works, but by trusting in what Christ accomplished on the cross.

The Mystery of the Rapture

The next great event in God's program is the rapture of the Body of Christ, the moment when all true believers are caught up to meet the Lord in the air.

Scripture: 1 Thessalonians 4:16-17 (KJV)

"For the Lord himself shall descend from heaven with a shout, with the voice of the archangel, and with the trump of God: and the dead in Christ shall rise first:

Then we, who are alive and remain, shall be caught up together with them in the clouds, to meet the Lord in the air: and so shall we ever be with the Lord."

Explanation:

This is not the Second Coming that happens later when Christ returns to earth to establish His kingdom.

The rapture is a heavenly event for the heavenly people, the Body of Christ.

It's called a mystery because it was revealed only through Paul.

Jesus mentioned resurrection in the Gospels, but not this "catching away" of believers to heaven before the tribulation.

Scripture: 1 Corinthians 15:51–52 (KJV)

"Behold, I shew you a mystery; We shall not all sleep, but we shall all be changed, In a moment, in the twinkling of an eye, at the last trump: for the trumpet shall sound, and the dead shall be raised incorruptible, and we shall be changed."

Explanation:

This is the blessed hope of every believer, not death, but transformation.

Those who have died in Christ will rise first, and those still alive will be instantly changed, receiving glorified bodies like Christ's.

Then together, we will be caught up to be with Him forever.

The 24 Elders: A Glimpse of the Raptured Church

In Revelation 4, John sees 24 elders already in heaven, clothed in white, wearing crowns, seated on thrones.

This is strong evidence that the rapture has already taken place by that point in prophecy.

Scripture: Revelation 4:4 (KJV)

"And round about the throne were four and twenty seats:

and upon the seats I saw four and twenty elders sitting, clothed in white raiment;

and they had on their heads crowns of gold."

Explanation:

These 24 elders represent the Church redeemed, rewarded, and reigning with Christ.

They are already in heaven before the judgments of Revelation begin, showing that believers have been removed prior to the tribulation.

The Judgment Seat of Christ (Bema Seat)

After the rapture, believers will stand before Christ not to be condemned, but to be rewarded for faithfulness.

Scripture: 2 Corinthians 5:10 (KJV)

> *"For we must all appear before the judgment seat of Christ; that every one may receive the things done in his body, according to that he hath done, whether it be good or bad."*

Explanation:

This is not a judgment of salvation.

Our sins were already judged at the Cross.

This judgment is for rewards symbolized by gold, silver, and precious stones, versus wood, hay, and stubble (1 Corinthians 3:12-15).

Our faithful service will be rewarded; our failures will be burned away.

But all believers will remain saved eternally secure in Christ.

The Return of Christ to Earth

After the rapture and the tribulation period, Christ will return with His saints to establish His kingdom on earth.

Scripture: Revelation 19:11, 14 (KJV)

> *"And I saw heaven opened, and behold a white horse; and he that sat upon him was called Faithful and True, and in righteousness he doth judge and make war...*
>
> *And the armies which were in heaven followed him upon white horses, clothed in fine linen, white and clean."*

Explanation:

We, the Body of Christ, will return with Him not to face judgment, but to reign with Him.

The twelve apostles will rule over the twelve tribes of Israel (Matthew 19:28),

while the Church, the Body of Christ, will reign with Him in heavenly places (Ephesians 2:6-7).

The Eternal State: Our Final Destiny

When sin and death are finally destroyed, we will live forever in perfect fellowship with God.

Scripture: Philippians 3:20–21 (KJV)

> *"For our conversation is in heaven; from whence also we look for the Saviour, the Lord Jesus Christ: Who shall change our vile body, that it may be fashioned like unto his glorious body, according to the working whereby he is able even to subdue all things unto himself."*

Explanation

Our final home is not on the earth but in the heavenly realm with Christ.

There we will serve, worship, and reign with Him in perfect peace, forever freed from sin, sickness, and death.

Closing Thought:

This is the glorious order of God's plan —

from the Cross to the Crown, from grace to glory.

It all centers around the risen Christ and the revelation given through His apostle Paul.

"For of him, and through him, and to him, are all things: to whom be glory forever. Amen." Romans 11:36

CHAPTER 6

The Law, Grace, And the Freedom We Have in Christ

One of the greatest misunderstandings in Christianity today is the difference between Law and Grace.

Many still try to mix the two — living partly under the old covenant and partly under the new.

But God makes it clear through Paul that we are no longer under the Law, but under Grace.

This chapter will show what that truly means — how we were once bound under the Law that could only condemn, and how Christ freed us through His finished work on the Cross.

1. The Purpose of the Law

The Law of Moses was holy and perfect — but it was never designed to save anyone.

It was given to show mankind the depth of sin and our need for a Savior.

Scripture: Romans 3:19–20 (KJV)

> *"Now we know that what things soever the law saith, it saith to them who are under the law, that every mouth may be stopped, and all the world may become guilty before God. Therefore, by the deeds of the law, there shall no flesh be justified in his sight, for by the law is the knowledge of sin."*

Explanation:

The Law was like a mirror — it showed our reflection but could not cleanse it.

It revealed sin, but it could not remove it.

Its purpose was to make humanity realize we could never be righteous on our own.

The Law said, "Do and live."

Grace says, "Believe and live."

2. The Law Was a Temporary Guardian

Before faith in Christ was revealed, Israel was kept under the Law as a schoolmaster — a temporary guardian until the promised Messiah came.

Scripture: Galatians 3:23–25 (KJV)

> *"But before faith came, we were kept under the law, shut up unto the faith which should afterwards be revealed.*
>
> *Wherefore the law was our schoolmaster to bring us unto Christ, that we might be justified by faith. But after that faith is come, we are no longer under a schoolmaster."*

Explanation:

A schoolmaster trains and disciplines children until they mature.

Once the child reaches maturity, the guardian is no longer needed.

Likewise, now that Christ has come and fulfilled the Law, we are no longer under that tutor.

We live by faith — not by rules and rituals, but by the indwelling Spirit.

3. The Weakness of the Law

The problem was not the Law itself, but the weakness of human flesh.

We could never live up to its perfect standard.

Scripture: Romans 8:3–4 (KJV)

> *"For what the law could not do, in that it was weak through the flesh, God sending his own Son in the likeness of sinful flesh, and for sin, condemned sin*

in the flesh. That the righteousness of the law might be fulfilled in us, who walk not after the flesh, but after the Spirit."

Explanation:

The Law demanded righteousness — Grace provides it.

Christ did what we never could — He perfectly obeyed God's Law, then took our punishment upon Himself.

Now His righteousness is imputed to all who believe.

4. Grace Frees Us from Condemnation

When we trust in Christ, we are no longer under condemnation.

God doesn't see our failures — He sees His Son's righteousness covering us completely.

Scripture: Romans 6:14 (KJV)

"For sin shall not have dominion over you: for ye are not under the law, but under grace."

Scripture: Romans 8:1–2 (KJV)

"There is therefore now no condemnation to them which are in Christ Jesus, who walk not after the flesh, but after the Spirit. For the law of the Spirit of life in Christ Jesus hath made me free from the law of sin and death."

Explanation:

Grace doesn't give us permission to sin — it gives us power not to.

41

Under the Law, we tried and failed.

Under Grace, Christ lives in us and gives victory.

It's not about performance — it's about position.

We are "in Christ," and therefore we are already accepted, forgiven, and sealed by the Holy Spirit.

5. The Cross Ended the Law's Dominion

When Christ died, the Law's demands were fully satisfied.

He nailed it to His cross.

Scripture: Colossians 2:13–14 (KJV)

"And you, being dead in your sins and the uncircumcision of your flesh, hath he quickened together with him, having forgiven you all trespasses;

Blotting out the handwriting of ordinances that was against us, which was contrary to us, and took it out of the way, nailing it to his cross."

Explanation:

The "handwriting of ordinances" refers to the Law — the record of our guilt that stood against us.

When Christ died, He wiped that record clean.

Every charge was canceled.

That's why believers no longer live under the commandments written on stone — we live by the Spirit written in our hearts.

6. Grace Brings Liberty, Not License

Paul often had to remind believers that freedom in Christ is not freedom to live carelessly — but to live righteously out of love.

Scripture: Galatians 5:13 (KJV)

> *"For, brethren, ye have been called unto liberty; only use not liberty for an occasion to the flesh, but by love serve one another."*

Explanation:

Under the Law, people obeyed because they had to.

Under Grace, we obey because we want to.

The Spirit changes our desires from the inside out.

When we understand what Christ did for us, love becomes our new motivation — not fear.

7. The Fruit of the Spirit Versus the Works of the Flesh

When a believer walks in the Spirit, the evidence shows in their life.

Scripture: Galatians 5:19–23 (KJV)

> *"Now the works of the flesh are manifest, which are these: Adultery, fornication, uncleanness,*

lasciviousness, Idolatry, witchcraft, hatred, variance, emulations, wrath, strife, seditions, heresies,

Envyings, murders, drunkenness, revellings, and such like... But the fruit of the Spirit is love, joy, peace, longsuffering, gentleness, goodness, faith, Meekness, temperance: against such there is no law."

Explanation:

The Law could only expose sin, but Grace produces fruit.

The Spirit works within us to bring forth these qualities, not by striving, but by surrendering to His guidance.

8. Our Identity Under Grace

When we believe the gospel — that Christ died for our sins, was buried, and rose again (1 Corinthians 15:3–4) — we are placed into the Body of Christ.

That becomes our new identity.

Scripture: 2 Corinthians 5:17 (KJV)

"Therefore if any man be in Christ, he is a new creature: old things are passed away; behold, all things are become new."

Explanation:

The Law saw us as sinners.

Grace sees us as sons and daughters of God.

We are no longer striving for approval — we already have it through Christ.

When God looks at the believer, He sees the righteousness of His Son.

9. Living by Grace Day to Day

The Christian life is not about keeping score or measuring up — it's about walking daily with the Lord who already finished the work.

Scripture: Philippians 1:6 (KJV)

> *"Being confident of this very thing, that he which hath begun a good work in you will perform it until the day of Jesus Christ."*

Explanation:

Grace began the work of salvation in us, and Grace will carry it to completion.

We live every day knowing that nothing — not even our failures — can separate us from the love of God (Romans 8:38–39).

That is true freedom.

That is the peace that passes understanding.

Closing Thought

The Law could never bring life — it only condemned.

Grace brings forgiveness, liberty, and the power of the Spirit.

We are no longer under the shadow of Mount Sinai, trembling under commandments.

We stand instead at the foot of the Cross, rejoicing in Christ's love and the freedom He purchased with His blood.

"Stand fast therefore in the liberty wherewith Christ hath made us free, and be not entangled again with the yoke of bondage." — Galatians 5:1

CHAPTER 7

Salvation What Happens to Us Once We Believe

(Scripture: KJV)

1. Justified, Romans 5:1:

"Therefore being justified by faith, we have peace with God through our Lord Jesus Christ."

Explanation:

God declares the believer righteous the moment faith is placed in Christ. This is a legal declaration, not a process.

2. Forgiven, Ephesians 1:7:

"In whom we have redemption through his blood, the forgiveness of sins, according to the riches of his grace."

Explanation:

All sins—past, present, and future—are forgiven through Christ's finished work.

3. Redeemed, Colossians 1:14:

"In whom we have redemption through his blood, even the forgiveness of sins."

Explanation:

The believer is bought out of the slave market of sin by Christ's blood.

4. Reconciled to God, Romans 5:10:

"For if, when we were enemies, we were reconciled to God by the death of his Son..."

Explanation:

The hostility between God and man is removed; peace is restored.

5. Born Again, John 3:3:

"Except a man be born again, he cannot see the kingdom of God."

Explanation:

Spiritual life begins instantly through regeneration, not human effort.

6. Made a New Creation, 2 Corinthians 5:17:

"Therefore if any man be in Christ, he is a new creature: old things are passed away; behold, all things are become new."

Explanation:

A new identity is given; the believer is now "in Christ."

7. Given Eternal Life, John 10:28:

"And I give unto them eternal life; and they shall never perish..."

Explanation:

Eternal life is a present possession, not a future reward.

8. Sealed by the Holy Spirit, Ephesians 1:13–14

"After that ye believed, ye were sealed with that holy Spirit of promise..."

Explanation:

The seal guarantees eternal security until redemption is complete.

9. Indwelt by the Holy Spirit, 1 Corinthians 6:19:

"Know ye not that your body is the temple of the Holy Ghost which is in you..."

Explanation:

God permanently dwells in the believer.

10. Baptized into the Body of Christ, 1 Corinthians 12:13:

"For by one Spirit are we all baptized into one body..."

Explanation:

The believer is placed into Christ and His Body, the Church.

11. Adopted as Sons, Galatians 4:4–5:

"To redeem them that were under the law, that we might receive the adoption of sons."

Explanation:

Believers receive full family status with God.

12. Accepted in the Beloved, Ephesians 1:6:

"Wherein he hath made us accepted in the beloved."

Explanation:

Acceptance is based on Christ, not performance.

13. Peace with God, Romans 5:1:

"We have peace with God through our Lord Jesus Christ."

Explanation:

The war between the sinner and God has ended permanently.

14. No Condemnation, Romans 8:1:

"There is therefore now no condemnation to them which are in Christ Jesus..."

Explanation:

Judgment for sin has already fallen on Christ.

15. Transferred into Christ's Kingdom, Colossians 1:13:

"Who hath delivered us from the power of darkness, and hath translated us into the kingdom of his dear Son."

Explanation:

A change of spiritual authority occurs instantly.

16. Positionally Sanctified, 1 Corinthians 1:2:

"To them that are sanctified in Christ Jesus..."

Explanation:

The believer is set apart unto God at salvation.

17. Made Complete in Christ, Colossians 2:10:

"And ye are complete in him..."

Explanation:

Nothing is lacking in the believer's standing before God.

18. Given Access to God, Ephesians 2:18:

"For through him we both have access by one Spirit unto the Father."

Explanation:

Direct access to God replaces distance and separation.

19. Written in the Book of Life, Revelation 20:15:

"Whosoever was not found written in the book of life was cast into the lake of fire."

Explanation:

The believer's name is recorded, securing eternal destiny.

20. Guaranteed Future Glorification, Romans 8:30:

"Whom he justified, them he also glorified."

Explanation:

Glorification is so certain that it is spoken of in the past tense.

CHAPTER 8

The Mystery of Israel's Blindness and God's Plan for the Ages

When God called Abraham, He promised to make him a great nation and to bless all families of the earth through his seed (Genesis 12:1–3). That seed, of course, would be Christ (Galatians 3:16).

But for centuries, God's plan focused on one nation— Israel. The Law, the prophets, the covenants, the promises, and even Christ's earthly ministry all centered on the nation that God chose to be His representative people on earth.

Yet something astonishing happened after Israel rejected her Messiah—a "mystery" that only Paul was given to reveal: Israel's blindness in part, until the fullness of the Gentiles comes in.

1. Israel's Rejection Foretold

Even before Christ's crucifixion, the prophets had spoken of a time when Israel's heart would be hardened, and their ears would not hear.

Isaiah 6:9–10 (KJV)

"And he said, Go, and tell this people, Hear ye indeed, but understand not; and see ye indeed, but perceive not.

Make the heart of this people fat, and make their ears heavy, and shut their eyes;

lest they see with their eyes, and hear with their ears, and understand with their heart, and convert, and be healed."

Explanation:

This prophecy began to unfold during Christ's ministry.

Jesus performed miracles, fulfilled prophecy, and declared Himself Israel's Messiah—yet the nation's leaders rejected Him.

Even after His resurrection, when Peter and the twelve offered the Kingdom once more in Acts 3:19–21, the nation still refused to repent.

2. The Fall of Israel and the Rise of Grace

When Israel's national rejection became complete (seen in Acts 7 when they stoned Stephen), God turned to an unlikely man—Saul of Tarsus.

That's when the transition began: the setting aside of Israel and the opening of a new dispensation—the age of grace.

Romans 11:11 (KJV)

"I say then, Have they stumbled that they should fall? God forbid: but rather through their fall salvation is come unto the Gentiles, for to provoke them to jealousy."

Explanation:

Israel's fall was not final, but temporary. Through her unbelief, God extended mercy to the Gentiles — not through Israel's rise as the prophets expected, but through her fall.

That's the great "mystery" Paul unfolds: God interrupted Israel's prophetic program to introduce something completely new — a Body of believers, both Jew and Gentile, united by faith in Christ alone.

3. The Mystery Revealed: Israel's Blindness in Part

Romans 11:25–27 (KJV)

"For I would not, brethren, that ye should be ignorant of this mystery, lest ye should be wise in your own conceits; that blindness in part is happened to Israel, until the fulness of the Gentiles be come in.

And so all Israel shall be saved: as it is written, There shall come out of Sion the Deliverer, and shall turn away ungodliness from Jacob:

For this is my covenant unto them, when I shall take away their sins."

Explanation:

Notice the phrase "blindness in part." Israel is not cast away forever. God's covenant promises are still sure. But for now—during this "dispensation of grace"—the nation as a whole is spiritually blind.

Once the Church (the Body of Christ) is complete and caught up at the Rapture, God will again turn His attention to Israel to fulfill her prophetic promises during the Tribulation and the Kingdom.

4. The Prophetic Program vs. The Mystery Program

It's important to understand the difference between these two programs:

Prophetic Program (Israel)	Mystery Program (Body of Christ)
Revealed since the world began (Luke 1:70)	Kept secret since the world began (Romans 16:25)
Earthly Kingdom promised	Heavenly inheritance promised
Christ as King and Messiah	Christ as Head of the Body

Salvation through Israel's rise	Salvation through Israel's fall
Focused on covenants and Law	Focused on grace and faith alone

5. God's Unchanging Faithfulness

Even though Israel is temporarily set aside, God's promises remain sure.

Paul reminds us that "the gifts and calling of God are without repentance" (Romans 11:29).

When this present age of grace concludes, God will resume His dealings with Israel.

The Tribulation will bring national repentance, and at Christ's return, Israel will finally recognize her Messiah and be restored.

Zechariah 12:10 (KJV)

"And I will pour upon the house of David, and upon the inhabitants of Jerusalem, the spirit of grace and of supplications:

and they shall look upon me whom they have pierced, and they shall mourn for him, as one mourneth for his only son, and shall be in bitterness for him, as one that is in bitterness for his firstborn."

Explanation:

This will be the moment Israel's blindness is lifted. The very One they rejected will be the One who redeems them.

At that time, prophecy will pick up right where it left off before Paul's ministry began.

6. The Church's Role During Israel's Blindness

During this present age, God is calling out a Body of believers from all nations—Jew and Gentile alike—to form the Body of Christ.

We are not part of Israel's prophetic plan but a new creation, reconciled to God through the cross.

2 Corinthians 5:17–19 (KJV)

"Therefore if any man be in Christ, he is a new creature: old things are passed away; behold, all things are become new.

And all things are of God, who hath reconciled us to himself by Jesus Christ, and hath given to us the ministry of reconciliation;

To wit, that God was in Christ, reconciling the world unto himself, not imputing their trespasses unto them; and hath committed unto us the word of reconciliation."

Explanation:

Our mission today is not to establish a kingdom on earth, but to preach the gospel of reconciliation—the message that salvation is available freely to all who believe.

When this Body is complete, Christ will call us home—the event Paul calls "the blessed hope" (Titus 2:13).

After that, God will resume His prophetic program with Israel.

7. God's Eternal Plan

From Genesis to Revelation, God's plan unfolds in perfect order:

1. Creation — God's purpose for man.
2. Fall — Man's rebellion.
3. Promise — God's covenant with Abraham.
4. Law — Israel's national covenant.
5. Grace — The hidden mystery revealed to Paul.
6. Rapture — Body of Christ taking out to meet Christ in air.
7. Tribulation — God's wrath and Israel's restoration.
8. Kingdom — Christ's thousand-year reign on earth.
9. Eternity — New heavens and new earth.

Each phase reveals more of God's mercy and wisdom.

What looks like delay is actually divine order.

In this present age, grace reigns—but soon, prophecy will resume.

8. Conclusion: A Perfect Plan in Two Programs

Paul's writings show us the beauty of God's plan:

He didn't abandon Israel; He simply paused her prophetic timeline to reveal His hidden purpose—the Body of Christ.

When this mystery program is complete, God will finish His promises to Israel, and all will be fulfilled in Christ—both in heaven and on earth (Ephesians 1:10).

Reflection

What a God of order and mercy we serve!

He works through history not by chance, but by divine design.

The blindness of Israel opened the door of salvation to the Gentiles—and one day, when the Church is caught away, Israel's eyes will be opened once again.

Until that day, we live as ambassadors of grace, holding forth the word of reconciliation in a world that still needs to hear.

CHAPTER 9

The Rapture: Our Blessed Hope and Heavenly Destiny

Throughout Scripture, God has revealed His purposes in order—the earthly promises given to Israel and the heavenly promises given to the Church, the Body of Christ.

Paul alone reveals a mystery never spoken before: the sudden transformation and catching away of believers—the Rapture.

This is not the "second coming" of Christ to the earth, but His appearing for His Body—to take us home to heaven before God resumes His prophetic dealings with Israel.

1. The Rapture Revealed Through Paul

Nowhere in the four Gospels do we find the doctrine of the Rapture.

Jesus spoke of His return to establish the Kingdom on earth—a visible, powerful event following the Tribulation.

But the Rapture was something kept secret until revealed to the Apostle Paul—another part of the "mystery" program committed to him.

1 Corinthians 15:51–52 (KJV)

"Behold, I shew you a mystery;

We shall not all sleep, but we shall all be changed,

In a moment, in the twinkling of an eye, at the last trump:

for the trumpet shall sound, and the dead shall be raised incorruptible, and we shall be changed."

Explanation:

This "mystery" is the instant transformation of believers—both those who have died and those still living—into glorified, heavenly bodies.

It's not a resurrection to life on earth, but to life in heaven.

The trumpet Paul speaks of is not the same as the trumpets of judgment in Revelation; it is the call for the Body of Christ to rise and meet our Head—the Lord Jesus.

2. The Blessed Hope

The Rapture is called our "Blessed Hope."

Titus 2:13 (KJV)

"Looking for that blessed hope, and the glorious appearing of the great God and our Saviour Jesus Christ."

Explanation:

Our hope is not in a political kingdom or a better world here below, but in being caught up to be forever with our Lord.

It's a hope rooted in promise, not fear—a deliverance from the wrath to come.

This event marks the completion of the Body of Christ. Once the last believer is added, the trumpet will sound, and the entire Body—dead and living—will rise together.

3. Comfort for Believers

The Rapture is not a doctrine of confusion or dread. Paul calls it a word of comfort.

1 Thessalonians 4:13–18 (KJV)

"But I would not have you to be ignorant, brethren, concerning them which are asleep,

that ye sorrow not, even as others which have no hope.

For if we believe that Jesus died and rose again, even so them also which sleep in Jesus will God bring with him.

For the Lord himself shall descend from heaven with a shout, with the voice of the archangel, and with the trump of God: and the dead in Christ shall rise first:

Then we which are alive and remain shall be caught up together with them in the clouds, to meet the Lord in the air:

and so shall we ever be with the Lord.

Wherefore comfort one another with these words."

Explanation:

The word "caught up" is from the Greek harpazo, meaning to seize or snatch away suddenly.

In Latin, it's rapturo — from which we get the word Rapture.

Those who have died "in Christ" will be raised first. Then those alive at that moment will be instantly changed and caught up together with them.

We'll meet the Lord in the air, not on the earth — proof that this event is separate from His return in glory.

4. Deliverance from the Coming Wrath

The Body of Christ is not appointed to wrath.

God's wrath will be poured out during the seven-year Tribulation, but before that begins, the Church will already be in heaven.

1 Thessalonians 1:10 (KJV)

"And to wait for his Son from heaven, whom he raised from the dead, even Jesus, which delivered us from the wrath to come."

1 Thessalonians 5:9–10 (KJV)

"For God hath not appointed us to wrath, but to obtain salvation by our Lord Jesus Christ,

Who died for us, that, whether we wake or sleep, we should live together with him."

Explanation:

These verses make it clear: the Church will not endure the wrath of God poured out during the Tribulation.

Just as Noah entered the ark before the flood and Lot was taken out before Sodom's destruction, so too will the Body of Christ be taken out before judgment begins.

5. The Heavenly Destiny of the Body of Christ

While Israel's hope is earthly—ruling with Christ in the Kingdom—the Body of Christ's hope is heavenly.

Philippians 3:20-21 (KJV)

"For our conversation is in heaven; from whence also we look for the Saviour, the Lord Jesus Christ: Who shall change our vile body, that it may be fashioned like unto his glorious body, according to the working whereby he is able even to subdue all things unto himself."

Explanation:

"Conversation" here means citizenship.

We are citizens of heaven, not of an earthly kingdom.

Our destiny is to reign with Christ in the heavenlies—fulfilling the heavenly side of God's plan, while Israel fulfills the earthly.

This is why Paul alone writes of being "caught up to the third heaven" (2 Corinthians 12:2) and why he speaks of believers as already "seated in heavenly places in Christ Jesus" (Ephesians 2:6).

6. Transformation, Not Resurrection Alone

At the Rapture, we won't merely be raised—we'll be transformed.

1 Corinthians 15:53–54 (KJV)

"For this corruptible must put on incorruption, and this mortal must put on immortality.

So when this corruptible shall have put on incorruption, and this mortal shall have put on immortality, then shall be brought to pass the saying that is written, Death is swallowed up in victory."

Explanation:

We will exchange these mortal, frail bodies for eternal, glorified ones—no more pain, sickness, or death.

This fulfills God's purpose in redeeming not only our souls but our bodies as well.

As Paul says in Romans 8:23, we "wait for the adoption, to wit, the redemption of our body."

7. After the Rapture: God's Program Resumes with Israel

Once the Body of Christ is removed, God's prophetic clock will start again.

The events of Daniel's 70th week—the seven-year Tribulation—will begin, focusing once again on Israel and the nations.

The Antichrist will rise, Israel will enter into covenant with him, and the world will be plunged into great deception and judgment—leading up to Christ's second coming to the earth in glory.

The Rapture, therefore, must occur before the Tribulation, because only then can God turn His full attention back to Israel.

8. Comfort and Motivation for the Church

Paul never uses fear to motivate believers—only hope.

Knowing that Christ could return at any moment gives urgency, joy, and peace to our lives.

1 Corinthians 15:58 (KJV)

"Therefore, my beloved brethren, be ye stedfast, unmoveable, always abounding in the work of the Lord,

forasmuch as ye know that your labour is not in vain in the Lord."

Explanation:

Because we know our destination, we can serve with confidence.

Every act of faith, every word of witness, and every kindness done in Christ's name has eternal value.

The trumpet could sound at any moment—and what a glorious day that will be!

9. The Blessed Reunion

Imagine that moment:

Loved ones raised from the grave, believers caught up alive, all meeting together in the clouds.

No more separation, no more sorrow, no more pain.

This is the promise that has sustained believers through centuries—the day when faith becomes sight, and we are forever with the Lord.

10. Conclusion: Our Hope Anchored in Heaven

The Rapture is not a fantasy — it is the next great event on God's calendar.

It completes the mystery revealed to Paul and fulfills God's promise to His heavenly people.

When that trumpet sounds, time as we know it will change forever.

The Body of Christ will rise, the age of grace will end, and God will once again resume His plan with Israel on earth.

Until that day, we wait — not in fear, but in faith — for the glorious appearing of our Savior, who loves us and gave Himself for us.

CHAPTER 10

Paul: The Prophet, The Apostle, And the Pattern for The Church

Throughout the Bible, God always raised up a man to deliver His message for each dispensation—Noah for the new world after the flood, Moses for the Law, and now Paul for the Dispensation of Grace.

Moses brought the Law down from Mount Sinai.

Paul brought grace and truth from the risen Christ in glory.

Just as Moses stood between God and Israel as a mediator, Paul stands as the chosen vessel through whom the heavenly message was given to the Body of Christ.

In this way, Paul can rightly be seen as both apostle and prophet—revealing mysteries no man had ever known.

1. Paul's Unique Calling

Before his conversion, Paul (then called Saul of Tarsus) was the fiercest enemy of Christ's followers. But God, rich in mercy, chose him for a purpose that would change the course of history.

Acts 9:15–16 (KJV)

"But the Lord said unto him, Go thy way: for he is a chosen vessel unto me,

to bear my name before the Gentiles, and kings, and the children of Israel:

For I will shew him how great things he must suffer for my name's sake."

Explanation:

God Himself called Paul, not man. He was chosen directly by the risen Christ—not during Jesus' earthly ministry, but from heaven after the resurrection.

That's why Paul's message is heavenly in nature. He didn't learn it from Peter or the Twelve, but by direct revelation from Christ.

Galatians 1:11–12 (KJV)

"But I certify you, brethren, that the gospel which was preached of me is not after man.

For I neither received it of man, neither was I taught it, but by the revelation of Jesus Christ."

Explanation:

This marks Paul as not only an apostle (a "sent one") but also a prophet—a man through whom God revealed new revelation for a new dispensation.

He didn't just proclaim what others had already known— he received and wrote mysteries that had been hidden in God since before the foundation of the world.

2. Paul: The Pattern for All Who Believe

Paul's conversion is more than a story of grace—it is a pattern for all who come to Christ under this age of grace.

1 Timothy 1:15–16 (KJV)

"This is a faithful saying, and worthy of all acceptation, that Christ Jesus came into the world to save sinners; of whom I am chief.

Howbeit for this cause I obtained mercy, that in me first Jesus Christ might shew forth all longsuffering,

for a pattern to them which should hereafter believe on him to life everlasting."

Explanation:

Notice Paul says, "in me first."

He was the first in a new order of believers—saved completely by grace, apart from the Law.

That's why we follow Paul as he followed Christ (1 Corinthians 11:1).

He is the model of the grace believer, showing that even the chief of sinners can become a vessel of mercy.

3. Paul as a Prophet: Revealer of the Mysteries

Moses gave Israel the Law written on stone.

Paul gave the Body of Christ revelation written on the heart—the mystery of grace, the Church, and our heavenly inheritance.

Romans 16:25 (KJV)

"Now to him that is of power to stablish you according to my gospel, and the preaching of Jesus Christ,

according to the revelation of the mystery, which was kept secret since the world began."

Explanation:

This mystery was not revealed to the prophets of old, nor to the Twelve Apostles during Christ's earthly ministry.

It was revealed first to Paul—making him both the apostle and the prophet of this new dispensation.

Paul's prophetic writings explain truths that complete God's program:

1. The Rapture (1 Thessalonians 4, 1 Corinthians 15)
2. The Body of Christ (Ephesians 1–3)
3. The Mystery of Israel's blindness (Romans 11)
4. The Indwelling of the Holy Spirit (1 Corinthians 6:19)

5. The heavenly inheritance of believers (Philippians 3:20–21)

All of these were hidden before Paul — but revealed through him.

4. The Foundation Layer: Paul the Master Builder

1 Corinthians 3:10–11 (KJV)

"According to the grace of God which is given unto me, as a wise masterbuilder, I have laid the foundation, and another buildeth thereon. But let every man take heed how he buildeth thereupon.

For other foundation can no man lay than that is laid, which is Jesus Christ."

Explanation:

Paul calls himself the "master builder" because he was entrusted with laying the foundation for the Church—the Body of Christ.

Every doctrine, practice, and hope we have as believers must be built on the foundation laid by Paul's gospel.

To mix in Israel's law or kingdom promises is to build on the wrong blueprint.

This makes Paul the Moses of the heavenly calling—the one through whom God gave instructions for His heavenly people.

5. Paul's Prophetic Foresight

Though his message was primarily for this age, Paul also foresaw what would happen after the Rapture—the rise of apostasy, false doctrine, and the final outpouring of evil.

2 Timothy 3:1–5 (KJV)

"This know also, that in the last days perilous times shall come.

For men shall be lovers of their own selves, covetous, boasters, proud, blasphemers, disobedient to parents, unthankful, unholy, Without natural affection, trucebreakers, false accusers, incontinent, fierce, despisers of those that are good, Traitors, heady, highminded, lovers of pleasures more than lovers of God; Having a form of godliness, but denying the power thereof: from such turn away."

Explanation:

This is prophetic truth for our time.

Paul foresaw our very generation — churches filled with religion but lacking spiritual power.

He warned believers to "rightly divide the word of truth" (2 Timothy 2:15) so they wouldn't be confused between Israel's earthly program and the Church's heavenly calling.

6. Paul's Message Was Final and Complete

Paul's last words, written in 2 Timothy, seal the revelation God gave him.

By the end of his ministry, he could say confidently:

Colossians 1:25–26 (KJV)

"Whereof I am made a minister, according to the dispensation of God which is given to me for you,

to fulfil the word of God;

Even the mystery which hath been hid from ages and from generations, but now is made manifest to his saints."

Explanation:

Paul's writings complete God's revelation for this present age.

That's why he could say he was given the dispensation "to fulfill the word of "God"—meaning to bring it to its full measure.

Everything we need for salvation, godliness, and hope in this age is found in Paul's epistles.

7. Paul's Legacy and Prophetic Role

Moses led Israel out of bondage to the Promised Land.

Paul leads believers out of religious bondage into grace and heavenly liberty.

In a sense, he is the modern-day Moses for the Body of Christ—not giving us law, but grace; not leading us to an earthly Canaan, but to our heavenly inheritance.

Paul's writings form the blueprint for how we are to live, serve, and look forward to Christ's return.

He's the voice of the risen Lord to His Body today.

8. Our Responsibility

If Paul's message is the voice of Christ for this age, then to ignore it is to miss God's instructions for today.

That's why we must study and teach his letters—Romans through Philemon—for they contain our doctrine, direction, and destiny.

2 Timothy 2:7 (KJV)

"Consider what I say; and the Lord give thee understanding in all things."

Explanation:

The Lord Himself gives understanding through the words of Paul.

When we study Paul's letters, we aren't just reading history—we're hearing the voice of the risen Christ speaking directly to His Body.

9. Conclusion: Paul, God's Chosen Vessel for the Heavenly Calling

Paul was more than a preacher.

He was the prophet-apostle of grace—chosen to reveal what God had kept hidden since the foundation of the world.

He completed the Word of God.

He unveiled the hope of heaven.

And he left us with the pattern of how to live by faith, not under law, but under grace.

His message is not just ancient text—it's the living voice of the glorified Christ to His Church today.

CHAPTER 11

Paul: The Modern-Day Moses — Leading Us Out of Religion and Into Grace

From the beginning of time, God has revealed Himself in stages—each dispensation showing another layer of His plan for mankind.

Moses was raised up to deliver Israel from bondage in Egypt, but Paul was raised up to deliver the world from the bondage of sin and religion.

Just as Moses led the people out of Egypt and into freedom under God's covenant, Paul leads the Church out of law and into grace—freedom under Christ.

1. Two Great Deliverers: Moses and Paul

God's purpose in Moses was earthly—a promised land for Israel.

God's purpose in Paul is heavenly—a promised home for the Body of Christ.

Both men met God personally.

Both received revelation directly from Him.

Both were entrusted with a divine message that changed the course of history.

Comparison	Moses	Paul
Met God Personally	In the burning bush (Exodus 3)	On the road to Damascus (Acts 9)
Given a message	The Law (Exodus 20)	The Gospel of Grace (Galatians 1:11-12)
Mediator for	Israel, the earthly nation	The Body of Christ, the heavenly people
Sign of calling	Face shining with God's glory	Eyes blinded by Christ's glory
Purpose	To bring Israel to the Promised Land	To bring the church to our heavenly home

Both men were rejected by their people the first time they appeared—Moses by Israel, Paul by Israel and religious leaders.

But in both, God's power was revealed in weakness and rejection.

2. Moses: The Lawgiver of the Old Covenant

Moses' ministry was necessary to expose sin.

The Law was holy, righteous, and good—but it could not save. It was a mirror showing man his guilt.

Romans 3:20 (KJV)

"By the law is the knowledge of sin."

The Law revealed what man could not do—it demanded perfection.

That's why Israel failed; the Law brought death, not life.

It showed that man's only hope was mercy and grace.

3. Paul: The Apostle of the New Covenant of Grace

When Christ appeared to Paul from heaven, the age of Law gave way to the age of Grace.

Through Paul, God offered a new way—righteousness apart from the Law.

Romans 3:21–22 (KJV)

"But now the righteousness of God without the law is manifested, being witnessed by the law and the prophets;

Even the righteousness of God which is by faith of Jesus Christ unto all and upon all them that believe."

Just as Moses gave the Ten Commandments, Paul gave what we might call the Ten Truths of Grace—the foundation stones of the Christian life.

Ten Truths of Grace (Paul's Gospel Blueprint)

1. Salvation by faith alone—not works (Ephesians 2:8–9)
2. Justification by Christ's finished work (Romans 5:1)
3. Indwelling of the Holy Spirit (1 Corinthians 6:19)
4. Unity in the Body of Christ—no Jew or Gentile (Galatians 3:28)
5. Freedom from the Law (Romans 6:14)
6. Heavenly citizenship (Philippians 3:20)
7. Sealed until the day of redemption (Ephesians 4:30)
8. A new identity "in Christ" (2 Corinthians 5:17)
9. Blessed with all spiritual blessings in heavenly places (Ephesians 1:3)
10. The hope of the Rapture—caught up to be with Christ (1 Thessalonians 4:16–17)

4. The Wilderness of Religion

Moses' people wandered in the wilderness for forty years because of unbelief.

In the same way, many today wander through the wilderness of religion—trying to please God by works instead of resting in grace.

They mix law and grace, flesh and spirit, and Israel's program with the Body's.

This confusion keeps believers from enjoying the liberty Paul taught.

Galatians 5:1 (KJV)

"Stand fast therefore in the liberty wherewith Christ hath made us free,

and be not entangled again with the yoke of bondage."

Like Moses, Paul's voice cries out to God's people: "Come out!"

Come out of law, out of works, out of ritual — and enter into the rest of grace.

5. Moses' Veil and Paul's Revelation

When Moses came down from Sinai, his face shone so brightly that Israel could not look at him—he had to cover his face with a veil.

That veil represented the blindness of Israel under the Law.

But Paul tells us that in Christ, the veil is taken away.

2 Corinthians 3:14–17 (KJV)

"But their minds were blinded: for until this day remaineth the same vail untaken away in the reading of the old testament; which vail is done away in Christ.

But even unto this day, when Moses is read, the vail is upon their heart.

Nevertheless when it shall turn to the Lord, the vail shall be taken away.

Now the Lord is that Spirit: and where the Spirit of the Lord is, there is liberty."

When a believer understands Paul's message, the veil comes off.

Grace is no longer a doctrine—it's a revelation that transforms the heart.

6. Paul's Exodus Message

Moses led Israel out of Egypt.

Paul leads believers out of religion—out of bondage to tradition and human effort.

Moses brought them through the Red Sea.

Paul brings us through the blood of Christ.

Moses gave them manna from heaven.

Paul reveals the Bread of Life—Christ in us, the hope of glory (Colossians 1:27).

Moses built the tabernacle.

Paul says we are the tabernacle—"the temple of the Holy Spirit."

7. Paul's Suffering: The Price of Deliverance

Both men paid a price for leading God's people.

Moses was criticized, doubted, and rejected.

Paul was beaten, stoned, imprisoned, and betrayed— even by those who claimed to follow Christ.

But like Moses, Paul never turned back.

He endured for the sake of those who would come to know the riches of God's grace.

2 Timothy 4:7–8 (KJV)

"I have fought a good fight, I have finished my course, I have kept the faith:

Henceforth there is laid up for me a crown of righteousness, which the Lord, the righteous judge, shall give me at that day."

Paul finished well—faithful to the end—because he knew his calling came directly from Christ in glory.

8. The Promised Land of Grace

For Israel, the Promised Land was Canaan—a land flowing with milk and honey.

For us, the Promised Land is not on earth but in heaven— a realm flowing with grace and glory.

Through Paul's message, we learn our true home is above— "seated with Christ in heavenly places" (Ephesians 2:6).

That is the destination of this new exodus.

9. Our Response: Follow Paul as He Followed Christ

Just as Israel followed Moses through the wilderness, believers today are called to follow Paul's teaching through this world.

Not because Paul was perfect — but because he was chosen as the pattern for this age.

To reject Paul's message is to wander in circles, never entering the rest of grace.

1 Corinthians 11:1 (KJV)

"Be ye followers of me, even as I also am of Christ."

Following Paul means walking by faith, resting in grace, and standing firm in truth—even when others compromise.

10. Conclusion: Grace Greater Than the Law

Moses' rod parted the Red Sea.

Paul's pen parted the veil between God and man.

Moses delivered a nation from slavery.

Paul delivered the world from religion.

Moses' people looked for an earthly kingdom.

Paul's people look for a heavenly one.

Both were chosen, both faithful—but Paul's ministry completed what Moses began.

Through him, we are led not to Mount Sinai, but to Mount Zion—not to thunder and fear, but to peace and grace.

Romans 6:14 (KJV)

"For sin shall not have dominion over you:

for ye are not under the law, but under grace."

Chapter 12

The Body of Christ: God's New Creation in Heaven and Earth

When God raised up the Apostle Paul, He revealed a mystery that had been hidden since the foundation of the world—the Body of Christ, a new creation made up of both Jew and Gentile, united by faith in Christ alone.

This was not a continuation of Israel's program.

It was a brand-new dispensation—a heavenly calling for a heavenly people.

1. God's Hidden Plan Revealed

For thousands of years, God dealt with Israel as a nation—giving them covenants, promises, and a land.

But when they rejected their Messiah, God revealed a new plan through Paul.

This plan had been "kept secret since the world began."

Romans 16:25 (KJV)

"Now to him that is of power to stablish you according to my gospel,

and the preaching of Jesus Christ, according to the revelation of the mystery,

which was kept secret since the world began."

That mystery is that Christ would create one new man—not Jew or Gentile, but a new spiritual Body united in Him.

Ephesians 3:5–6 (KJV)

"Which in other ages was not made known unto the sons of men,

as it is now revealed unto his holy apostles and prophets by the Spirit;

That the Gentiles should be fellowheirs, and of the same body,

and partakers of his promise in Christ by the gospel."

Before Paul, nobody knew about this Body—not the prophets, not the apostles, not even the angels (1 Peter 1:12).

It was a secret hidden in God Himself until the risen Christ revealed it directly to Paul.

2. One Body, One Spirit, One Hope

The Body of Christ is not an organization — it's an organism, a living temple where Christ Himself dwells.

Every believer is joined to Him the moment they believe the Gospel of Grace.

1 Corinthians 12:12–13 (KJV)

"For as the body is one, and hath many members, and all the members of that one body, being many, are one body:

so also is Christ.

For by one Spirit are we all baptized into one body, whether we be Jews or Gentiles,

whether we be bond or free; and have been all made to drink into one Spirit."

This is not a baptism with water—it is a spiritual baptism performed by the Holy Spirit, placing us "in Christ."

In that moment, we become one with Him and with all who belong to Him.

3. A Heavenly People, Not Earthly

Israel's hope was the earthly kingdom promised to Abraham and David.

But the Body of Christ's hope is heavenly—our citizenship is above.

Philippians 3:20 (KJV)

"For our conversation [citizenship] is in heaven;

from whence also we look for the Saviour, the Lord Jesus Christ."

That means our blessings, inheritance, and destiny are all spiritual and heavenly.

We are not promised land, riches, or thrones on earth— we are promised a seat in the heavenlies, ruling with Christ.

Ephesians 2:6 (KJV)

"And hath raised us up together, and made us sit together in heavenly places in Christ Jesus."

This is the difference between Prophecy and Mystery— Israel's story was foretold by prophets; the Church's story was hidden until Paul.

Comparison	Israel (Prophecy)	The Body of Christ (Mystery)
Revealed	Since the world began	Hidden since the world began
Sphere	Earthly Kingdom	Heavenly Places
Message	Law and Works	Grace through Faith
Mediator	Moses	Paul

Hope	Messiah ruling on Earth	Christ returning for His Body
Identity	Nation of Priests	New Creation
Future	Millennium Reign	Rapture & Heavenly Glory

4. The New Creation

When a person believes Paul's Gospel—that Christ died for our sins, was buried, and rose again (1 Corinthians 15:1–4)—God does something miraculous.

He creates something entirely new inside us.

2 Corinthians 5:17 (KJV)

"Therefore if any man be in Christ, he is a new creature: old things are passed away; behold, all things are become new."

This "new creature" is not a cleaned-up version of the old man—it's a brand-new spiritual being joined to Christ Himself.

That's why Paul can say, "It is no longer I who live, but Christ lives in me" (Galatians 2:20).

We no longer live for God in our strength—we live from God, in His Spirit.

5. The Unity of the Spirit

The Body of Christ is not divided by denomination, title, or nationality.

We are one in spirit—equal at the foot of the cross.

When Paul wrote, "There is neither Jew nor Greek, bond nor free, male nor female," he was declaring the death of all fleshly distinctions in this new creation.

In God's eyes, there's only one identity that matters— "in Christ."

Ephesians 4:4–6 (KJV)

"There is one body, and one Spirit, even as ye are called in one hope of your calling;

One Lord, one faith, one baptism, One God and Father of all, who is above all, and through all, and in you all."

6. The Role of Christ as Head

In this new creation, Christ is the Head of the Body.

He directs, nourishes, and strengthens every member.

Just as a body cannot function without the brain, the Church cannot function apart from its Head.

That's why Paul emphasized spiritual connection over physical ritual.

Colossians 2:19 (KJV)

"And not holding the Head, from which all the body by joints and bands having nourishment ministered, and knit together, increaseth with the increase of God."

The modern Church often forgets this truth.

We build programs and traditions, but Christ alone is the Head who gives life.

7. Christ's Body Will Be Raptured

When the last member of the Body of Christ is added, the Church will be caught up to meet the Lord in the air.

This is our blessed hope—the Rapture.

1 Thessalonians 4:16–17 (KJV)

"For the Lord himself shall descend from heaven with a shout, with the voice of the archangel, and with the trump of God:

And the dead in Christ shall rise first:

Then we which are alive and remain shall be caught up together with them in the clouds, to meet the Lord in the air: and so shall we ever be with the Lord."

When that moment comes, the Body will be complete.

Christ will take His Church home, and God's prophetic program for Israel will resume during the Tribulation.

8. Our Calling: Walk Worthy of the Body

Knowing we are part of this heavenly Body should change the way we live on earth.

Paul wrote that we should "walk worthy of the vocation wherewith ye are called" (Ephesians 4:1).

That means we live not in guilt, but in gratitude.

We serve not to earn favor, but because we already have it.

We forgive others because we've been forgiven.

Our conduct becomes a reflection of the grace that saved us.

9. Conclusion: The Mystery Completed

When Paul revealed the Body of Christ, he was showing God's masterpiece — the greatest display of grace in all creation.

Through us, God is teaching even the angels what His grace looks like.

Ephesians 3:10 (KJV)

"To the intent that now unto the principalities and powers in heavenly places

might be known by the church the manifold wisdom of God."

Moses gave the Law to Israel.

Christ gave Grace to Paul.

And Paul gave the message of the Body to us—the Church, His heavenly people.

We are the culmination of God's eternal plan—His new creation, His workmanship, His Body.

Ephesians 3:21 (KJV)

"Unto him be glory in the church by Christ Jesus throughout all ages, world without end. Amen."

CHAPTER 13

The Heavenly Destiny of The Church and The Coming Kingdom of Christ

From Genesis to Revelation, the Bible tells one great story—how God restores His creation through two programs:

an earthly kingdom promised to Israel, and a heavenly inheritance revealed through the Apostle Paul for the Body of Christ.

These two programs are separate, yet perfectly united under the Lord Jesus Christ—"the Head of all things."

1. Two Realms, One Lord

When Christ ascended into heaven, He was exalted "far above all heavens, that He might fill all things" (Ephesians 4:10).

God gave Him authority over both realms—heaven and earth.

Through Israel, He will one day rule the earth from Jerusalem.

Through the Church, His Body, He will rule the heavenly realm.

That's why Paul wrote in Ephesians 1:10:

"That in the dispensation of the fulness of times he might gather together in one all things in Christ,

both which are in heaven, and which are on earth; even in him."

This verse summarizes all of God's purpose:

Heaven and earth reconciled, united in Christ—the true King and Lord of all.

2. The Earthly Hope — Israel's Promised Kingdom

From Abraham onward, God promised an earthly kingdom.

Israel would inherit the land, the throne, and the blessings of peace under their Messiah.

Jeremiah 23:5–6 (KJV)

"Behold, the days come, saith the Lord, that I will raise unto David a righteous Branch,

and a King shall reign and prosper, and shall execute judgment and justice in the earth.

In his days Judah shall be saved, and Israel shall dwell safely:

and this is his name whereby he shall be called, THE LORD OUR RIGHTEOUSNESS."

This kingdom will come after the Tribulation, when Christ returns to the Mount of Olives (Zechariah 14:4).

The apostles—the twelve—will sit on twelve thrones, judging the twelve tribes of Israel (Matthew 19:28).

This is the fulfillment of Israel's earthly hope.

But the Church, the Body of Christ, has a very different destiny.

3. The Heavenly Hope — The Body of Christ's Eternal Home

Paul revealed that believers in this present dispensation are not part of Israel's earthly kingdom but part of a heavenly calling.

Our home, our citizenship, and our inheritance are all above the heavens.

Colossians 3:1–4 (KJV)

"If ye then be risen with Christ, seek those things which are above,

where Christ sitteth on the right hand of God.

Set your affection on things above, not on things on the earth.

For ye are dead, and your life is hid with Christ in God.

When Christ, who is our life, shall appear, then shall ye also appear with him in glory."

This is not symbolic—it is literal.

We will appear with Him in heavenly glory, with resurrected bodies fit for eternity.

Paul calls this our "blessed hope."

Titus 2:13 (KJV)

"Looking for that blessed hope, and the glorious appearing of the great God and our Saviour Jesus Christ."

We are not waiting for signs or judgments—we are waiting for a Person.

The trumpet will sound, and the Church will be caught up to meet Him in the air (1 Thessalonians 4:16–17).

That's when the Body of Christ is complete.

4. The Judgment Seat of Christ — Our Eternal Rewards

After the Rapture, believers will appear before the Judgment Seat of Christ—not for condemnation, but for reward.

2 Corinthians 5:10 (KJV)

"For we must all appear before the judgment seat of Christ;

that every one may receive the things done in his body, according to that he hath done, whether it be good or bad."

Paul explains this further in 1 Corinthians 3:12–15, comparing our works to materials:

"Now if any man build upon this foundation gold, silver, precious stones, wood, hay, stubble;

Every man's work shall be made manifest...

If any man's work abide... he shall receive a reward.

If any man's work shall be burned, he shall suffer loss: but he himself shall be saved; yet so as by fire."

This shows that even though salvation is secure, our service will be tested.

Faithful believers will receive crowns of reward— incorruptible glory that will last forever (1 Corinthians 9:25; 2 Timothy 4:8).

Those crowns are not for pride—they are for worship, to cast before His throne in gratitude.

5. The Great White Throne — For the Unbelieving Dead

The Great White Throne Judgment, found in Revelation 20:11–15, is not for believers.

It is for the lost of all ages—those who rejected God's grace.

"And whosoever was not found written in the book of life was cast into the lake of fire."

Believers will never appear there because their sins were judged at the cross.

Our judgment took place at Calvary—Christ bore our punishment in full.

That's why Paul could write with confidence:

Romans 8:1 (KJV)

"There is therefore now no condemnation to them which are in Christ Jesus."

6. Christ's Return with His Church

When the Rapture and heavenly rewards are complete, Christ will return with His saints at the end of the Tribulation to establish His millennial kingdom on earth.

This fulfills both heavenly and earthly purposes.

The Church—the Body—will reign with Him in the heavens, while Israel will reign on the earth under the New Covenant.

2 Timothy 2:12 (KJV)

"If we suffer, we shall also reign with him: if we deny him, he also will deny us."

In the end, every realm of creation—heaven, earth, and under the earth—will bow before the Lord Jesus Christ.

Philippians 2:9–11 (KJV)

"Wherefore God also hath highly exalted him, and given him a name which is above every name:

That at the name of Jesus every knee should bow, of things in heaven, and things in earth, and things under the earth;

And that every tongue should confess that Jesus Christ is Lord, to the glory of God the Father."

7. God's Eternal Plan Complete

In the end, God's two purposes—Israel's earthly kingdom and the Church's heavenly inheritance—will merge under one Head: Christ.

All rebellion will be gone, and eternity will begin.

Then shall come to pass the words Paul wrote:

1 Corinthians 15:28 (KJV)

"And when all things shall be subdued unto him,

then shall the Son also himself be subject unto him that put all things under him, that God may be all in all."

8. Our Eternal Destiny

For the believer, eternity means being with Christ—forever loved, forever secure, forever home.

We will serve Him, worship Him, and share in His glory as His heavenly family.

And just as Israel will dwell safely in her land, the Body of Christ will dwell joyfully in the heavenlies—the two programs, finally united in perfect harmony.

Ephesians 1:6 (KJV)

"To the praise of the glory of His grace, wherein He hath made us accepted in the Beloved."

Closing Reflection

Paul's message is clear:

We are not waiting for wrath — we are waiting for redemption.

We are not of this world — we are seated with Christ above.

And one day soon, the trumpet will sound, and faith will give way to sight, as we meet our Savior face to face.

Revelation 22:20

"Even so, come, Lord Jesus."

CHAPTER 14

The Mysteries Revealed to The Apostle Paul

Deuteronomy 29:20 *"The secret things belong to the LORD our God, but the things that are revealed belong to us and to our children forever, that we may do all the words of this law."*

Paul's ministry is unique because Christ revealed to him truths that had been hidden, "kept secret since the world began" (Romans 16:25).

These doctrines were not known by the prophets, by Israel, or by the Twelve apostles during Jesus' earthly ministry.

Below are all of Paul's major mysteries clearly listed and explained.

1. The Mystery of the Body of Christ

Scriptures: Ephesians 3:1–6; Colossians 1:24–27; 1 Corinthians 12:12–27

What the mystery is:

That Jew and Gentile are now joined together in one new man, one Body, not under the Law, not separated by covenants, but united by grace through faith.

Explanation:

This Body is a brand-new creation, not Israel, not Gentile, but something that never existed before Pentecost or the prophets. Every believer is placed into this Body by the Holy Spirit.

Why it matters:

This is the foundation of the Church Age and explains why our hope, identity, and destination are heavenly.

2. The Mystery of the Indwelling Christ ("Christ in You")

Scriptures: Colossians 1:26–27; Galatians 2:20; Romans 8:10

What the mystery is:

The risen Christ personally indwells every believer.

Explanation:

Under the Law, God dwelled in temples made of stone. Now He lives in the believer—something never revealed before Paul.

Why it matters:

This truth gives assurance, identity, and spiritual power. Our life is literally in Christ.

3. The Mystery of the Gospel of Grace

Scriptures: Acts 20:24; Ephesians 3:2; Romans 3:21–28; 1 Corinthians 15:1–4

What the mystery is:

Salvation apart from the Law, apart from works, apart from Israel—based solely on Christ's death, burial, and resurrection.

Explanation:

The prophets foretold the Messiah's suffering, but the meaning of the cross—as payment for the whole world—was revealed clearly only to Paul.

Why it matters:

This is our gospel today. It is how we are saved.

4. The Mystery of the Rapture

Scriptures: 1 Corinthians 15:51–53; 1 Thessalonians 4:13–18

What the mystery is:

A generation of believers will be transformed instantly and caught up to meet Christ in the air before God resumes His program with Israel.

Explanation:

This was never in Old Testament prophecy. Israel's hope is the kingdom on earth; the Body of Christ's hope is being taken to heaven.

Why it matters:

It establishes our heavenly destiny and separates Church Age doctrine from Israel's earthly kingdom.

5. The Mystery of Israel's Blindness

Scriptures: Romans 11:25–27

What the mystery is:

Israel is temporarily blinded until the "fullness of the Gentiles" comes in.

Explanation:

Israel's rejection of Christ did not cancel their promises; it postponed them. God paused Israel's prophetic program to begin the Age of Grace.

Why it matters:

Explains why Israel is not currently central in God's program — but will be again.

6. The Mystery of the One New Man (Joint-Heirs)

Scriptures: Ephesians 2:14–18; Ephesians 3:6

What the mystery is:

In the Body of Christ, Jew and Gentile share the same spiritual status, blessings, and access to God.

Explanation:

Under the Law, Gentiles were "strangers." Under grace, they are equal members in Christ.

Why it matters:

This reveals our unity and equal standing—something unthinkable under the Law.

7. The Mystery of Godliness

Scriptures: 1 Timothy 3:16

What the mystery is:

Christ, God in the flesh, revealed through the church to the world.

Explanation:

This describes the revelation of Christ's nature and work—seen in the incarnation, resurrection, ascension, and proclamation to the nations.

Why it matters:

It explains how God reveals Himself today, not through Israel, but through the Body of Christ.

8. The Mystery of the Faith

Scriptures: 1 Timothy 3:9; Romans 16:25

What the mystery is:

A complete system of doctrine for the Church Age, centered on grace, not the Law.

Explanation:

Paul calls it "my gospel" because it was entrusted to him to proclaim to the world.

Why it matters:

This defines how we live, walk, and understand our relationship with God.

9. The Mystery of the Will of God

Scriptures: Ephesians 1:9–10

What the mystery is:

God's plan to gather all things — heavenly and earthly — under Christ.

Explanation:

Israel receives earthly promises; the Body of Christ receives heavenly promises. In eternity, Christ reigns over both realms.

Why it matters:

It reveals the big picture of God's eternal purpose.

10. The Mystery of the Resurrection Body

Scriptures: 1 Corinthians 15:35–58

What the mystery is:

Believers will receive glorified bodies suited for heaven, not earth.

Explanation:

These bodies will be incorruptible, immortal, and spiritual—unlike Israel's earthly resurrection hope.

Why it matters:

It aligns with our heavenly calling and explains our eternal state.

11. The Mystery of Lawlessness

Scriptures: 2 Thessalonians 2:7–8

What the mystery is:

The spirit of lawlessness is already at work in the world but is restrained until the Body of Christ is removed.

Explanation:

This explains the rising rebellion against God, the future Antichrist, and why evil is presently limited.

Why it matters:

Shows God's control over history and the future tribulation.

12. The Mystery of Gentile Salvation

Scriptures: Ephesians 3:1–8; Romans 11:11–13

What the mystery is:

God would offer salvation to Gentiles apart from Israel's kingdom.

Explanation:

Before Paul, Gentile blessing depended on Israel's rise. Under grace, God blesses Gentiles directly through Paul's gospel.

Why it matters:

Explains why the Gentile world has responded to the gospel for 2,000 years.

EPILOGUE

The Blessed Hope

As I come to the end of this book, my heart overflows with gratitude and awe for what the Lord has revealed through His Word. When I first began studying Scripture deeply, I never imagined how clear and consistent God's plan would become when viewed through the eyes of the Apostle Paul—our apostle for this present age of grace.

Through the years of study, prayer, and reflection, I've learned that God's Word never contradicts itself—it unfolds. The Lord's plan for Israel and His plan for the Body of Christ are distinct, yet both are rooted in His mercy and faithfulness. Israel looks forward to her earthly kingdom under Christ's reign, while we, the Body of Christ, are called to a heavenly inheritance. Both reveal the glory of our Lord Jesus Christ, who is the Head of all things in heaven and on earth.

I've also come to understand that even our trials have a divine purpose. God used my battles with cancer and my time on the edge of life itself to show me that every breath is a gift. My survival was no accident—it was grace. The same grace that saved Paul, that called me, and that offers eternal life to all who believe.

As I reflect on my journey—through sickness, healing, loss, and faith—I realize how powerfully the Holy Spirit teaches through both Scripture and experience. The same God who raised Jesus from the dead raised me from a hospital bed more than once, and for one reason only: to share this message of grace, hope, and truth.

When the rapture occurs, we who are in Christ will be caught up together with Him in glory. No judgment awaits us—only reward at the Judgment Seat of Christ, where our faithfulness will be tested as by fire. The things done for His glory will remain as gold, silver, and precious stones, while the rest will be burned away. Yet even then, we will still be His—forever secure, forever redeemed, forever with the Lord.

If anything in this book helps one person come to a clearer understanding of God's plan of salvation and the unique message given to Paul for the Body of Christ, then all the effort, study, and prayer have been worth it.

Until that glorious day when we hear the trumpet sound, may we stand firm in faith, rest in grace, and rejoice in the blessed hope of our calling in Christ Jesus.

"Looking for that blessed hope, and the glorious appearing of the great God and our Saviour Jesus Christ."